MOONPOWDER

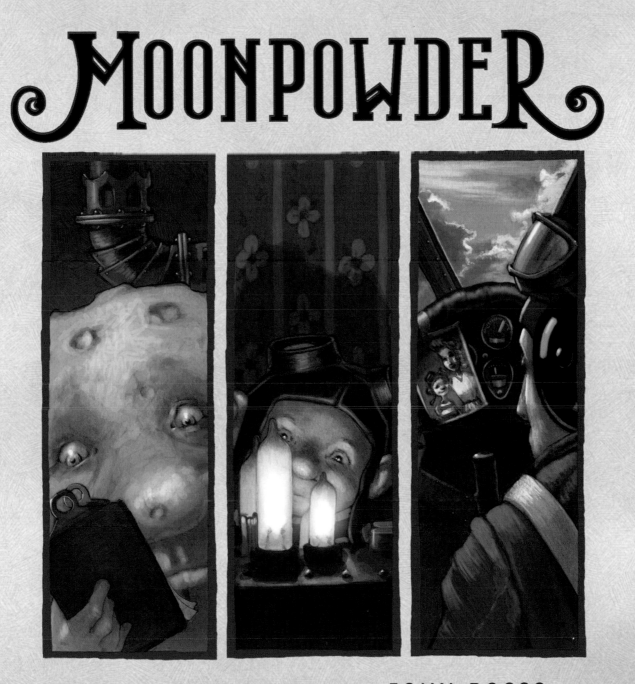

STORY AND PICTURES BY JOHN ROCCO

HYPERION BOOKS FOR CHILDREN
NEW YORK

AN IMPRINT OF DISNEY BOOK GROUP

this book is dedicated
to the children of soldiers
everywhere.

CAP'N JACKS
AVIATOR GOGGLES

ONLY
49¢

THE

RECORD MONTH
YANKS HALF MILE FROM
DUREN

Printed in Singapore
First Edition
3 5 7 9 10 8 6 4 2
F850-6835-5-11105
Library of Congress Cataloging-in-Publication Data on file.
ISBN-13: 978 1-4231-0011-9
ISBN-10: 1-4231-0011-5
Reinforced binding
Visit www.hyperionbooksforchildren.com

Eli carefully turned the knob on the radio. It crackled to life.

"ELI TREEBUCKLE," his mother said, flicking off the radio with a loud *CLICK*. "It's past your bedtime."

"Shucks, Mom, I just fixed it."

"And I see you fixed the fan and the vacuum cleaner, but it's still time for bed." As she kissed him on the forehead, her voice softened. "Good night, my little fix-it man. Sweet dreams."

Eli shuffled off to his room, silently dreading each step.

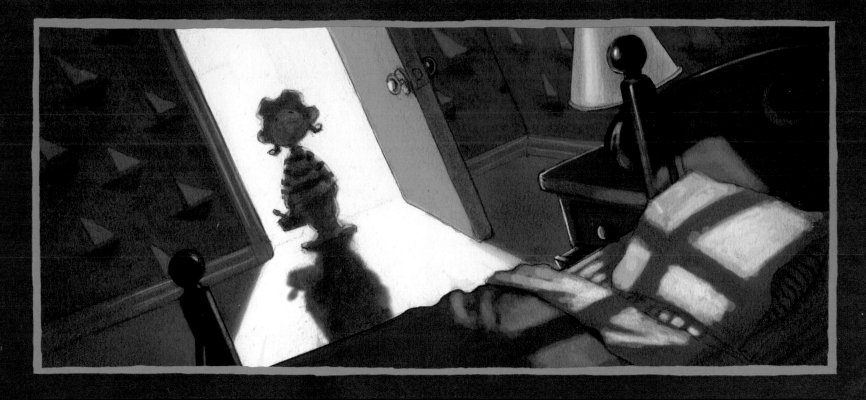

I never have sweet dreams. Never.

That was the one thing Eli couldn't fix. For months he'd been having the same nightmare.

It was always dark and booming. He'd climb a mountain of junk, desperately searching for something he could never find. And each time, he would fall.

"That's it!" he huffed. "I'm never going to sleep again!"

Working on his helio-rocket-copter was just the thing to keep Eli awake.

He could stay up for hours, tinkering with his inventions.

"Can't sleep?" asked a voice.

"Who in the Sam Hill are you?" Eli asked the large luminous man at his window.

"Call me Mr. Moon," the man said, examining his notebook. "And you're Eli Treebuckle, 'fixer of all things fixable.' How come you can't sleep?"

"I don't *want* to sleep."

"Nightmares, huh?" Mr. Moon scratched down a note. "Not getting enough Moonpowder."

"What's Moonpowder?" Eli edged over to the window.

"Why, Moonpowder is a magical marvel, a masterful miracle, a mystical masterpiece. . . ." Mr. Moon brought his voice to a whisper. "It helps everyone have sweet dreams."

"I haven't had a sweet dream in months," Eli sighed.

"That's why I'm here. The Moonpowder factory has been on the blink lately, and I thought *you* might be able to fix it."

Mr. Moon stepped back to reveal a life-size helio-rocket-copter in the backyard.

"Hey! That's my invention!" Eli scrambled out the window toward the ship.

"I thought you might like it."

The cool night air whistled in Eli's ears as they flew up over the town.

"IT WORKS!" Eli gasped.

"Of course it works." Mr. Moon smiled. "You designed it."

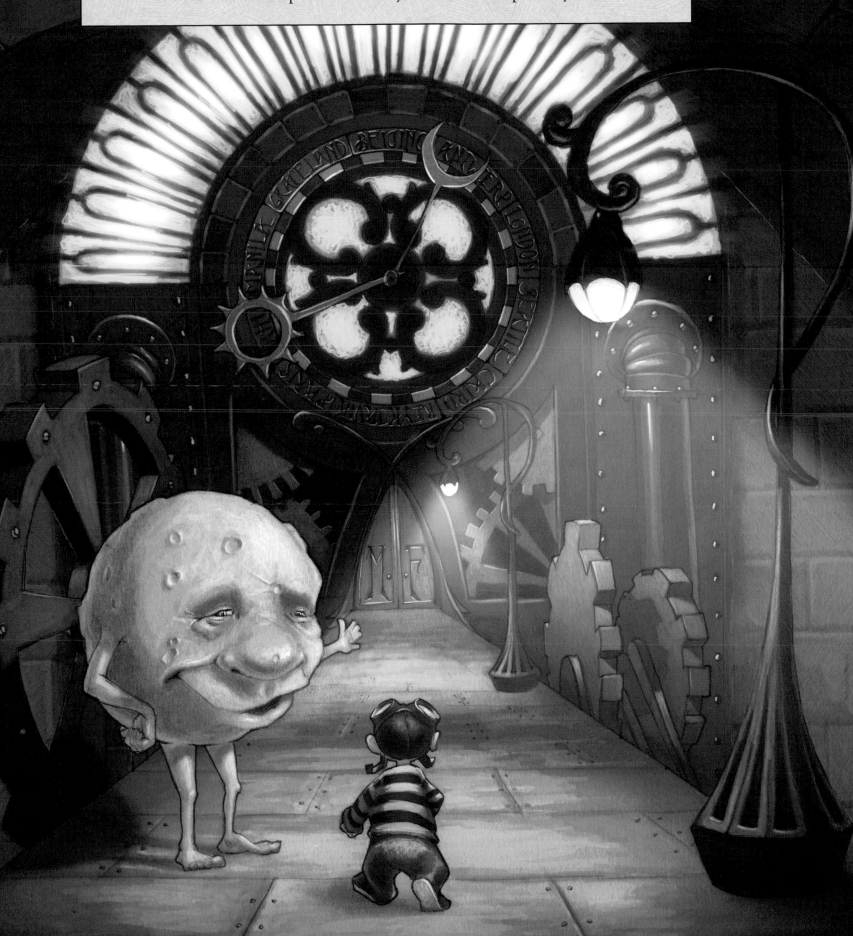

Inside, hundreds of mechanical gizbots were frantically adjusting valves and turning dials.

"It's about time!" A small gizbot glided toward them.

"What's the situation, Giz?" Mr. Moon scanned the chart the gizbot handed him. "Oh, dear. Not good. Not good at all."

"Hello." Eli smiled, offering his hand.

Giz trained his eye-bulbs on Eli. "Is *that* the fixer?"

"Yes, yes, Eli Treebuckle, the fixer of all things fixable!" Mr. Moon patted Eli on the back. "We have no time to lose."

"But I don't know how anything in this place works."

Giz shoved a thick book into Eli's arms. "You can start by reading this."

CHAPTER III
THE
MOONPOWDER
FACTORY

AN

OVERVIEW

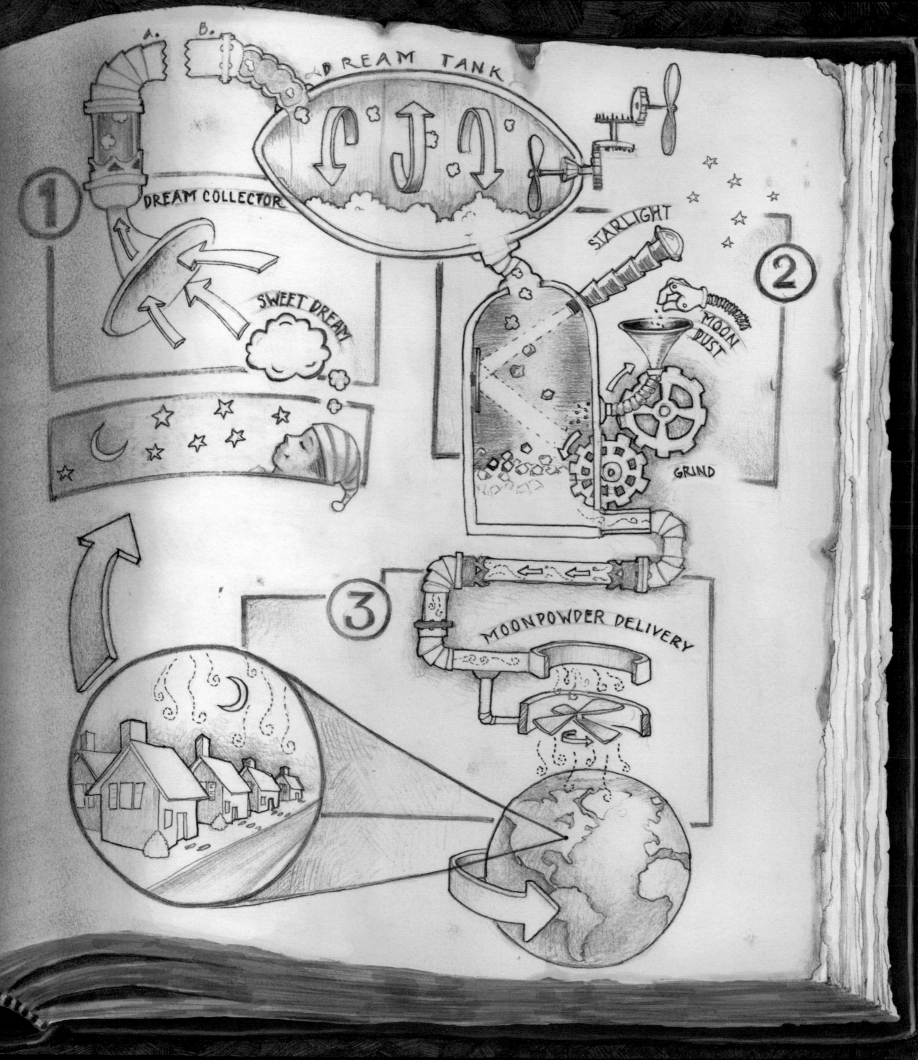

"So if I fix the factory, I'll have sweet dreams?"

"Absolutely, positively!" Mr. Moon beamed.

Eli inspected every inch of the factory, checking gauges, tightening valves, and tapping on dials.

"What's this one?" Eli rapped his knuckles against a rusty metal vat. A hollow echo filled the room.

"*This*," Mr. Moon said, "is the Dream Tank."

"Well, it's empty, and I can't fix that," Eli said, wiping his greasy hands on his pajamas.

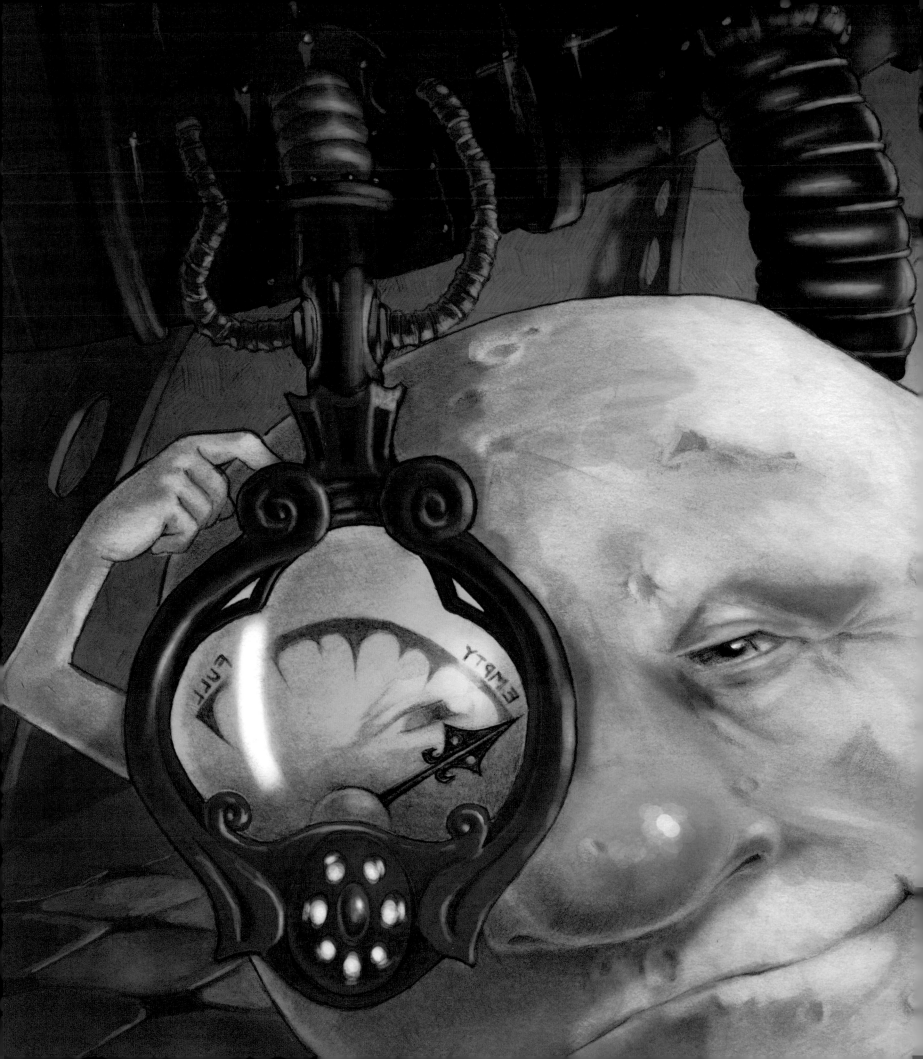

"No dreams left! This is terrible, just terrible!" Mr. Moon mopped his brow.

"Can't you just get some more?" Eli asked.

"It's not that simple," Mr. Moon explained. "Without dreams, we can't make Moonpowder, and if we can't make Moonpowder, no one will have sweet dreams."

"And the chance of someone having a sweet dream without Moonpowder is six hundred and twenty-three million to one," Giz added.

"But you must have a backup supply or something," Eli offered.

"That's right!" Mr. Moon lit up. "The Special Emergency Dream Kit!"

"But that's in Mother Nature's closet," Giz interrupted. "You remember what happened last time we went in there."

Mr. Moon rolled his eyes. "It was an accident."

"What happened?" Eli asked.

"I left open a freezer full of snowstorms," Mr. Moon said.

"In the middle of *summer*!" Giz laughed. "Since then, we haven't been allowed to go in."

Mr. Moon focused on Eli. "But he can."

Seconds later, the three of them were rushing down to the basement toward Mother Nature's closet.

"When you get inside, just find a small red box," Mr. Moon said excitedly. "That's the Special Emergency Dream Kit. It has the last remaining pinch of Moonpowder. With that, *you* can have a sweet dream and restart the factory."

Reluctantly, Eli pushed open the heavy door. Looming in front of him was an enormous mountain of boxes, crates, and barrels. Thunder rumbled from inside a trembling trunk. Lightning flashed from another. Eli's heart sank.

"I can't do this!" he called back to them. "It's just like my nightmare."

"That's why you *have* to do it," Mr. Moon said. "If we don't get that box, everyone will have nightmares . . . forever."

Eli swallowed hard and started to climb. A thick layer of dust made it difficult to read the labels on the boxes.

As he climbed higher, his arms began to ache. Just when he thought he couldn't go on, he saw the small red box. It was barely beyond his reach. He stretched out toward it. His legs began to twitch. The boxes beneath him started to shift. And then Eli fell.

In a flash, Eli read the label on the box lid in his hands.

TORNADO DISPENSER:

use with caution.

"HOLD ON!" Mr. Moon yelled.

"TO *WHAT*?" Eli cried out as he spun around faster and faster inside the closet.

The tornado ripped open crates and broke open jars. Fall leaves, spring flowers, and icicles whipped past his head. Rainbows and lightning lit up the vortex.

Then, just as quickly as it began, the tornado was sucked through a vent in the floor. Eli dropped like a rock.

When he came to, he heard whispering.

"We shouldn't have sent him in there. This is dreadful, just dreadful." Mr. Moon's voice cracked.

"Mother Nature is not going to be happy about this," said Giz.

"Never mind her, what about Eli?"

Eli was inside a large trunk. With his last bit of strength, he pushed open the lid. That's when he saw the small red box resting at his feet.

"I GOT IT!" he yelled.

"ELI!" Mr. Moon ran over and hugged Eli as tears of relief streamed from his eyes. "I knew you could do it! I knew it all along."

"That kid's got moxie!" Giz laughed. "Now let's go collect that sweet dream."

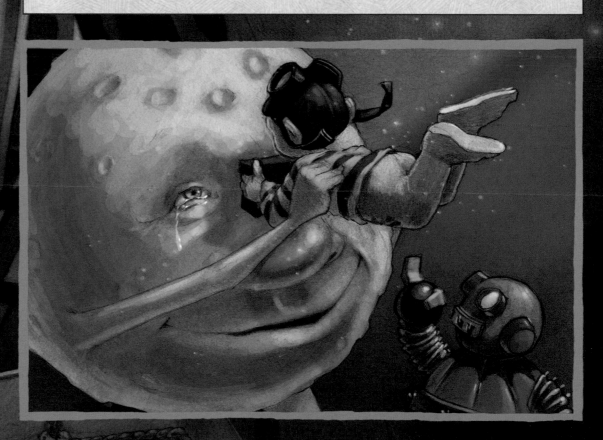

Back upstairs, Eli climbed into the dream bed. Mr. Moon reached into the red box and pulled out a tiny velvet bag tied with a satin ribbon.

"Are you ready to have a sweet dream?"

"More than ready. I'm beat."

Mr. Moon carefully put his hand into the bag. His eyes suddenly went wide.

"What's wrong?" Giz asked.

"There's no Moonpowder left," Mr. Moon gasped. "*Not one grain!*"

That was the last thing Eli heard. His head fell back onto the soft pillow, and he was asleep . . .

. . . and having a sweet dream.

When Eli woke, he was back in his own bed. The sun was shining.

I did it! I must have restarted the factory!

Just then he heard his name being called from somewhere outside. He rushed out the door, expecting Mr. Moon and Giz to be there. But it was someone else.

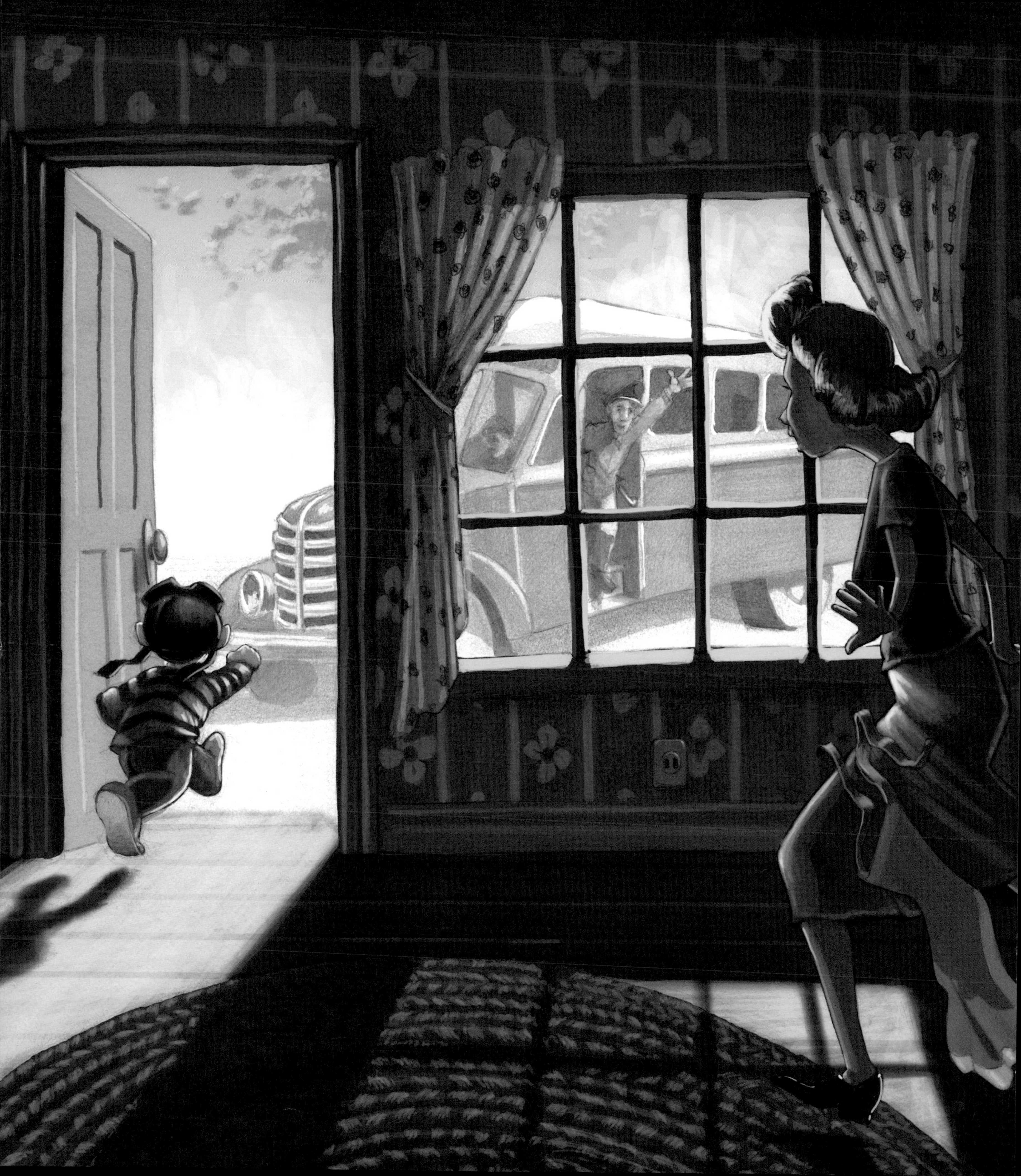

"I hear you have been fixing everything around here lately." His dad smiled.
"Not *everything*," Eli said. "Some things just fix themselves."